SPARE PARTS

RELICS OF THE ANCIENTS

M.G. HERRON

Ever since they became refugees, Elya Nevers collected bot parts.

He didn't know exactly how the idea had first come to him. Even his memory of it as an idea was nebulous. Elya couldn't recall the concepts of *collecting* and *bot parts* ever pairing in his brain before they fled their cliffside solar farm in the night. He barely had time to throw a change of clothes and his tab into his rucksack before his mother dragged him and his two older brothers out the door and into the darkness. In their flight to the city, there had been no time for such thoughts.

He didn't remember making a conscious decision to be a collector when the four of them shoved their way onto an orbital transport shuttle, fighting against the panicked crowds, nor when the shuttle blazed through the planet's atmosphere. It was hard to focus on much of anything when the seat was rattling so hard he thought his brains would shake out of his mouth and splash all over his only pair of boots.

When they passed into space and the shuttle stabilized, Elya looked down and noticed that his left hand was bleeding where he gripped a gold-tinted gear in his palm. Its reflective surface, even smeared with blood, calmed him for some reason. As he studied its finely cut teeth, noting its purposeful shape, he realized that he must have picked up the gear along the way, although he couldn't for the life of him remember where or when. Its golden color was distinctive compared to the dull grey of the utility bots they sometimes rented as extra hands to help during harvest time on the farm. Elya didn't really have a use for the gear, since the Nevers had never been able to afford a bot of their own—especially not a gold-plated one. *But I do have room in my rucksack*, he thought, and decided to keep it.

When the shuttle reached the limit of its range, the refugees were transferred to a Mammoth long-hauler. Elya had plenty of time to contemplate his new habit of collecting bot parts during their harried spaceflight, while his mother clutched her bead necklace and muttered prayers under her steaming breath. When she finally slept, he and his brothers listened to their frightened fellow refugees speculate how long it would take the Imperial Fleet's starfighters to find them and guide them to safety. (Answer: twenty-three days, Galactic Standard Time.)

While they waited, the slow-moving longhauler drifted on minimum viable power—life support only. They kept the passenger cabin above freezing, but not by much, and the pilot had the ship's comms beacon off so that the Kryl couldn't track them. The only lights found among the stowaways were hoarded by the few people smart enough to pack electric torches, or wealthy enough to own personal servant bots in their previous lives. Elya had never seen luxury bots like these up close before, but he saw that only a few of them were finished in the same shade of gold as his gear.

He stayed warm by searching the passenger cabin for more spare parts. The behavior became as much a part of him as his darkly tanned skin or his long, dextrous fingers. When he was alone in the dark, Elya would pass the time counting and cataloging his growing collection by feel. Since the gear, most of the spare parts he gathered had been found on the floor of the longhauler. Others he looted from a closet full of damaged Mammoth repair bots. Once, he won an aluminite power switch playing aleacc against a rich merchant's son. The stunned look on the kid's face when Elya rolled doubles three times in a row was his greatest source of pleasure on the seemingly endless journey. Elya placed the switch carefully in his rucksack. At night, when sleep wouldn't come, he would take it out and flip the mechanism back and forth, back and forth.

But nothing cleared or calmed his mind like the feel of the golden gear against his skin. It was the only thing he had left that reminded him of home.

[2]

An overwhelming stench struck Elya like a fist halfway down the airlock connecting the Mammoth longhauler with the space station. The smell was sour and heavy and so thick it made him gag. He looked down and coughed, someone jostled him, and he staggered sideways under the weight of his pack.

His older brother caught him before he could fall. "Easy, little brother," Arn said.

Arn was the eldest of the three Nevers boys—tall and calm and always ready with a word of encouragement. Had those lines in his forehead always been etched so deep? Elya hadn't seen Arn's face in the light often during their spaceflight, but he didn't think so. The ship's lights had only come on for the first time when the longhauler got clearance to dock with the space station. Elya's eyes had been adjusting to the overwhelming brightness ever since.

"Try breathing through your mouth," Arn said. "It still reeks, but you won't notice as much."

Elya nodded. He kept walking and tried not to vomit up the vitamins sitting like dead power cells on the floor of his hollow stomach. By pretending he didn't have a nose and keeping his eyes on Rojer's back instead of the vacuum of dead space on the other side of the transparent walls, he made it to the end of the airlock's gangway without puking.

It didn't take long to discover the source of the stench—a crowd of sweaty, unwashed people filled the vast hangar in which they emerged. They covered the floor, even spilling over into the demarcated area where smaller spaceships docked, unloaded, or refueled. At the far end from where they stood, an arched doorway led to the rest of the station. An enormous line trailed from that opening. Elya didn't need anyone to explain to him why it was so crowded; it was obvious: the space station's shuttle bay had been transformed into a refugee intake center.

Elya followed his brothers and his mother to a speck of empty floor where they wouldn't get jostled by the many moving bodies, or block the way of those still coming out behind them. The airlock they had come through was one of a dozen such mouths, each pouring out innumerable unkempt refugees from several different vessels—people from Yuzosix, just like them. Tens of thousands had already arrived and were making their vague way through the line—and then through the door that led to the rest of the station, and the end of this part of their journey. Elya didn't know what awaited them on the other side of that door, but almost anything was better than living in perpetual darkness on the Mammoth.

Elya's mother studied the crowd, then sighed. She looked each of her boys in the eye. "Stay close, all right? Watch out for each other."

"Where are we going now?" Rojer whined.

"They have to process us," Mom said. "To know how many people made it out." *Out alive. Out of Yuzosix.* "It shouldn't take long."

Arn nodded and smiled, to reassure their mother. It worked less well than it normally did. Elya scuffed a shoe against the floor. His mother smiled back, and it looked forced. Rojer continued to look sullen and angry—but that wasn't all that unusual.

Elya tightened the straps of his rucksack, then put his hand into his pocket and ran his fingers over the golden gear's teeth. Their hard edges, the satisfying way they rose and fell as he traced them, kept him from showing his anxiety to the rest of the Nevers clan.

"And you," Mom said, pointing a long bony forefinger at Elya so that he couldn't pretend she was talking to Rojer or Arn instead. "Don't wander off.

We're not on the longhauler anymore. We don't know anything about these people, and I don't want to lose you."

She took another deep breath and sighed, more heavily this time.

Together, they waded into the sea of people. Mom led the way, with Rojer right behind her kicking at debris and vitamin wrappers on the floor. Elya came next, and Arn brought up the rear.

Not everyone seemed to be in the same rough shape as them. A large group accompanied by several security bots emptied luggage from small private ships to their right. Past them, a group of desert dwellers in brightly colored robes sat cross-legged on the floor around an oscillating hologram of a multi-armed deity who led them in prayer. A pair of old men whispered and passed a bottle between them, making faces as they swallowed. Most of the people he saw seemed to be from Yuzosix, but not all.

The less fortunate waited in a smaller line that formed fifty meters from the bigger one. Each person who got to the front was scanned for ID, and then doled out rations by a plump man in an Imperial uniform. He wielded a handheld holodisplay connected to the ship's main computer and an expression that reminded Elya of Rojer when someone stepped on his toes. The steward was flanked by two security guards of his own—human soldiers, not bots. These men and women bore blaster rifles in their arms, and attentively studied the people in line. Like the steward, their uniforms were a rich blue trimmed in crimson. Similarly uniformed guards, each wearing a helmet that concealed their face, were spaced out around the edge of the hangar.

As they walked, Elya's attention was drawn like a magnet to a third small theater that had formed in a far corner of the hangar. People there weren't lined up so much as gathered around, shoulder to bot to shoulder. Everyone waiting in the crowd had a decommissioned bot either held in their arms or wheeled on a maglev dolly at their side. A few of the personal servant bots were standing and operational, but most were not.

Everyone seemed to be vying for the attention of a giant man in a red jumpsuit. He had enormous muscular arms and shoulders, and long dark hair gathered with rubber bands into thick ropes. The man lifted his muscular arms and rained three blows down on something that echoed with a hollow metallic gong each time he struck it. He switched the tool in his hand, slapped a mask down over his face, and touched the flame of a welding torch to the object; an explosive hiss reverberated into the hangar's high ceilings. As people waiting jostled and shoved for prime spots near the front of the gathering, Elya caught a glimpse of the bot he was working on—a personal servant bot finished in red-tinted silver. The tri-star Imperial insignia was painted in black on the bot's chest.

"Watch it, runt!" Rojer snapped, shoving Elya sideways. Rojer was always calling Elya names, but this time he thought he might have actually deserved it. Elya had been so caught up studying the machinist and the anxious crowd that had gathered to take advantage of his talents that Elya didn't notice he had bumped into his brother.

But even if he was in the right, Elya hated it when Rojer was mean to him. Rojer hadn't seemed to have the heart to be nasty on the longhauler, where there was no light and no one knew if they would be rescued or starve to death as they drifted through space. Here, in the light and noise of the space station, it was different. Rojer felt emboldened. Heads snapped toward them, and under the weight of hundreds of eyes, Elya felt his face flush with shame.

"Cut it out, both of you," Arn snapped. He stepped between them, trying to defuse the situation. The smirk on Rojer's face caused Elya to see red. He knew what Roj was thinking: *Arn to the rescue*. Well, not this time.

He lunged around Arn and grabbed Rojer by the thick curls their mother loved so much. Yanking down, he was glad to hear his brother shout in pain and fright, and flail about, slapping at Elya's wrists.

But he had his long fingers gripped tight about his brother's hair, and the pain he felt at his brother's blows wasn't nearly as scary as it used to be. Not after their flight from Yuzosix. That experience had reset his pain tolerance to a new plateau in ways Elya was only now, in this moment, coming to understand.

One of Rojer's flailing arms caught Elya's rucksack, and he managed to pull so hard that Elya stumbled forward. Hair ripped, Arn shouted, and Elya pitched to the ground, scraping his chin against the rough metallic floor of the hangar.

He fully expected the weight of his pack to crush the wind from his chest, or perhaps protect him from Rojer as his brother fell on his back, but neither of those things happened. Instead, his pack felt light as air. A musical tinkling sound made Elya's blood run cold.

Lifting his head, Elya watched in helpless horror as the contents of his rucksack tumbled forth, between the legs and under the feet of the crowd. Not just blankets and his toothbrush and dirty underwear, but the bot parts he'd so secretively and carefully stowed. Nuts and bolts scattered and fell between cracks in the floor. Tubes and wires were stomped underfoot and ground down. A ball bearing met the toe of a shoe at speed and rocketed away, lost forever in a dense patch of people to his right.

Worst of all, the golden gear fell out of his

pocket, and momentum set the precious piece to rolling. It wobbled as it found its balance, then came upon a slight slope and rolled away, nimbly dodging between pairs of legs whose owners Elya couldn't see and didn't care to know.

He realized by then that Rojer's flailing arms must have caught the zipper and opened his pack, but Elya only had eyes for the gear. He struggled to his knees, having forgotten all about Rojer until a sharp pain blossomed against the back of his skull, and a weight from above tried to smear him across the grated metal flooring of the hangar.

"Get off!" Elya shouted, "Rojer, getoffame!"

"I didn't know you were such a packrat, Elly."

Though it took all the air left in his lungs, Elya cried, "Don't call me that, you sniveling little twerp!"

"*Elya!*" his mother screeched, as she finally noticed what was happening behind her. How she could be more alarmed about Elya's choice of words than his short-tempered and obnoxious brother attacking him for no reason was beyond him. His mother's abiding love and forgiveness of Rojer's insufficiencies was one of the Seven Galactic Wonders.

Arn set his feet on either side of Elya's head, balled Rojer's clothes in both of his huge hands, and hauled their brother bodily into the air with a roar of effort. Rather than face his mother or watch Rojer be manhandled by Arn—as much pleasure as that *always* gave him—Elya scrambled to his feet and ran in the direction the gear had gone. He never took his eyes off it. The gear rolled with beautiful efficiency, its finely cut teeth allowing it to tumble unheeded over the hangar floor.

The golden gear turned between the legs of a boy, who missed his chance at grabbing it, and then beneath the frayed skirts of an old lady before it finally fetched up against a rubber sole of someone's boot.

The boot attached to the rubber sole was made of expensive, oiled leather. Tucked into their fur-lined tops were clean, crisply ironed pants—made of the expensive fiber the Nevers family had grown in their solar farm, to sell to the merchants in Yuzo City. As Elya's eyes traveled up, he realized that the expensive boots and pants belonged to the merchant's son, the same snot-nosed brat he'd won the power switch from in a game of aleacc onboard the Mammoth. He had known the kid was taller than him, but now that he was properly lit and standing next to a gleaming golden servant bot, Elya saw that the boy was older than Elya by at least a few years, and well-muscled in ways that Elya's body, just barely edging into puberty, was not yet even capable of becoming.

With a smirk like a dull knife, the merchant's son caught Elya's forlorn gaze, then bent down and picked up the gear. The boy twisted the golden cog in the light. Then, without breaking eye contact, he placed it inside his tunic, next to his skin.

Elya's fists tightened into balls. This boy had a servant bot of his own. What in all the livable worlds did he need with a lonesome gear? Besides, that gear belonged to Elya. He'd found it, so it was his by rights. More importantly, it came from Yuzosix, so it had more sentimental value than all the other parts he'd collected put together. Elya shoved his way through the crowd, ignoring the sounds of scratching and arguing coming from Arn, who was still tangled up with Rojer, and ignoring his mother's cries as she tried to pull the two apart.

Elya closed the distance to the merchant's son in a few quick strides.

As it became apparent where Elya was headed, the servant bot stepped forward and put himself between Elya and the snot-nosed boy, whose name was... What was his name? Elya couldn't remember. It didn't matter.

"That's mine," Elya said, pointing an accusing finger at the boy's tunic where he had tucked the gear away.

"What is?" the boy said, touching an artistic hand to his chest and putting on his best confused face.

Elya barely recognized the fury seething through his bones and causing him to curl his toes in his boots. Words shot straight from his aching heart to his tongue, bypassing his brain completely. "You know what," Elya growled.

The boy looked around, then up at the bot. "I really don't. Do you, Ambit?"

The bot cocked its head and glanced between the two of them. "I am no longer certain, Master Kristoph."

Oh, that's right. The boy had introduced himself as Kris when they played aleacc together on the Mammoth. "Kris, please… I—I need that back."

"Or what?" he asked, his tone mocking.

"I just need it back."

Kristoph shrugged. "Not my problem," he said, dropping the feigned ignorance now that it no longer benefited him. "You have one of mine, and now I have one of yours. It seems to me like we're even."

"I won that power switch fair and square, and you know it. You didn't win the gear. You just stole it. It's not yours!"

Kristoph shrugged and studied his perfectly buffed nails. How had this rich brat managed to stay so *clean* on the Mammoth, when Elya felt as if he'd been covered in a layer of dirt for a month? "Finders keepers."

This sent Elya into a rage, partly because he used the same justification to keep the gear in the first place. But there had been no encounter with the gear's owner when he discovered it. For all Elya knew, the golden gear had materialized out of thin air. It was just *there*, in his hands, absent of any question of ownership. Elya had felt like it belonged to him the first moment he laid eyes upon it and was careful to keep it private so that no such questions arose. By the time they were clear of the planet's atmosphere, the gear really was his. There was no possibility of finding the owner. It was his by rights. Finders keepers.

Powered by this sudden anger, Elya leaped forward to snatch the gear straight out of Kristoph's tunic. But the servant bot was faster. A golden arm shot out, acting like a barricade that kept Elya at a safe and harmless distance.

Someone screamed. Only after bruising his knuckles and chipping his fingernails clawing and thrashing at the bot—and failing to gain so much as a centimeter—did Elya realized the animal noise was coming from his own throat.

"What is the meaning of this?" A fat, bearded man with a triangular hat bellowed, marching up from behind Kristoph.

"I don't know, father," Kristoph said. "This underfed gutter rat attacked me for no reason. If Ambit wasn't here…"

"Guards!" The man bellowed. "Guards!"

Elya froze. Guards were bad. Guards were real bad. *Where did Arn and Rojer go? Mom?* Looking around, he saw nothing but a sea of strange faces crowded tightly around, watching the drama unfold with cruel anticipation. In the distance, two blaster-wielding soldiers peeled away from the wall and began to wade through the crowd in their direction.

Feeling pressured as he saw his window of opportunity closing, Elya became indignant. "He stole my gear. I'm just trying to get it back."

"Gear?" Kristoph's father, the merchant, demanded in a brusque manner, crossing his arms and glaring at his son. "Is this true?"

"What?" Kristoph scoffed. "No, of course not."

"I don't see any gear, boy. You're a liar."

"No!" Elya felt his face heat up. "No, I'm not. That's not true. He's the liar!"

At the insult to his son, the older merchant's broad forehead smoothed out. His face went stony and his arms dropped to his side.

"Ambit, down," the merchant said in a flat voice.

The golden bot dropped his arms to his side and made an electronic wheezing sound that came out like a sigh. His head dipped, almost as if he felt slightly guilty—Elya made that same gesture himself when his mother grilled him about something he shouldn't have been doing—then straightened.

Elya braced himself. But the blow he expected never came.

"Little brother," Arn said. The relief in his voice was palpable. "Come on, Elya. You can't keep wandering off like that."

"I didn't wander off!" Elya snapped. The indignation that had built up in the frustrating conversation with Kristoph spilled out all over his brother. He didn't mean to get angry at Arn, but it wasn't right. Arn smiled down at him sadly, as if at someone mentally inadequate. It filled Elya with both shame and confusion because he wasn't inadequate. That was Rojer, if it was anyone.

Before Elya could say anything else, his mother appeared, all smiles and apologies. "Please forgive my son," she said. "It's been a long journey, sir, and we're all very tired."

The merchant's face softened at the sight of his mother. Elya noticed the way the man's eyes traveled up and down her body. He relaxed and smiled broadly. "It's no trouble."

"Thank you, sir," she said. "We'll be going now."

Arn slowly backed away, dragging Elya with him.

"But he stole my gear!"

"Quiet."

"But—"

"Shh!"

The rich merchant turned to talk to the guards, who had finally arrived, shrugging elaborately and laughing in his belly. Elya couldn't hear his words, but his expression seemed to say, *Boys will be boys, you know?* The guards followed the Nevers clan with their eyes but didn't pursue them.

Elya had no choice. He followed Arn and was

shepherded along by his mother. When they got back to where Rojer was waiting, he was holding Elya's pack. It had been repacked with his belongings and what bot parts Rojer had been able to retrieve from the floor nearby. Elya snatched the rucksack out of his brother's hands and didn't speak to anyone for a long time.

3

After three days, Elya barely noticed the stink of unwashed people anymore, at least not unless he accidentally got up close to one. And he tried very hard to avoid that.

The space station was shaped like a star, five arms of five levels each. It was called Solaran's Bridge on the Imperial starmap Elya found on his tablet, and the cyclopedia described it as a pit-stop between the Yuzo chain of star systems and the viridian spiral arm. Or it used to be. Imperial news-feeds all reported that the Fleet had pulled back to safety after the rescue. The volume of space between Yuzosix and Yuzotwelve was under Kryl control now. So, Elya supposed, Solaran's Bridge was no longer a pit-stop to anywhere people were safe. He wasn't afraid to admit how glad he was that the plan was to relocate his family, eventually. Their journey wasn't over quite yet.

For now, the Nevers were given a cramped little room in the corner of what Elya thought of as the north point of the star. In space there was no north, no true direction at all. It simply felt like that because of the way the design of interlocking arrows on the floor all pointed in a single direction. "It's so you always know where you are, and never get lost," Mom explained.

"I don't get lost," he insisted.

"It's still good to know," she said.

Arn insisted that Mom slept in the bottom bunk, while the boys rotated between the top bunk and the floor. The room was a cramped closet compared to the space they once shared in their cliffside dwelling —and certainly less room than Elya needed to get a break from Rojer's constant, low key torment—but it was more than they had on the Mammoth, and at least it had lights and a door that closed. For that, he was grateful.

Rumor had it that the researchers and staff had started to refer to the station as Solaran's *Ditch*, especially the lower levels given over to the refugees. To Elya, the halls seemed less crowded than the hangar, yet it became known that a hundred thousand people were currently breathing the same recycled air.

Even knowing the odds, it still took several days

of searching for Elya to admit that his chances of recovering his golden gear had gone to zero. Despite seeing phantoms of Kristoph's dull-knife smirk around every corner, the merchant's family must have been able to afford quarters in a better part of the station than the Nevers. Though Elya kept his eyes peeled, he never saw the other boy.

He blamed Kristoph for stealing the gear, of course. And Rojer too. But he blamed himself most of all. After Yuzosix, Elya should have known better than to let himself get attached to anything.

As they were getting ready for bed one night, Rojer whined, "How long do we have to stay here?" Rojer got to have the bed the previous night. Now that it was Arn's turn, he was acting like a baby about it.

"Not long," Mom said. "This is temporary."

"Temporary until when?"

"Until they find a place to resettle us."

"I hope it's in the viridian spiral arm," Arn said. "I heard they have settler's moons there. Imagine if we were granted land to start a new farm." Of the three boys, Arn enjoyed farming the most. He found a quiet joy in hard labor that Elya never managed to muster. Arn was tall and strong, and even back on Yuzosix every commented on how his lanky frame had begun to gather muscle. He looked just like their father, people said. Compared to Arn, Elya was a runt. He was built more like their mother, quick and dextrous, but small and lean.

Rojer snorted. "And you know what they say about the girls on settler's moons."

"Stop it, Rojer," their mother chided, but Arn was already blushing.

Due to the influx of refugees on the station and the scarcity of essential supplies, food and water continued to be strictly rationed. Elya managed to save enough of his drinking water to wash himself over the sink every couple days. It wasn't the same as taking a hot shower, but it was better than smelling himself all the time. He wished Rojer would do the same. His brother had always hated washing up, and Elya was still too mad at him to give him the dignity of letting him know how badly he reeked.

Unlike his sour middle brother, Elya was determined to make the most of their stay. The station was packed to the gills with refugees from his home-world, and there was a lot to see. Yuzosix had been a big planet and he'd only ever seen a small corner of it, so many of the people he passed in the halls appeared foreign to him. They dressed in different styles of clothing and spoke in dialects he'd never heard before. All the exotic wonder they represented made Elya restless. Fortunately, once the Nevers settled in, his mother gave him more slack to wander.

Under one condition. Arn had to accompany him; only then was Elya allowed to explore.

Arn rolled his eyes in front of Rojer, but he went willingly enough. After all, Rojer hadn't been wrong about their responsible big bro. A hundred thousand exotic people meant exotic women, and Arn wanted to meet them all.

It didn't take long for Elya to fill up his rucksack with newly discovered treasures. He had a talent for spotting bot parts. A small glint on the floor caught his eye while they were strolling along a corridor in the southeast corner of the station.

"What's that one?" Arn asked.

Elya picked it up, noting the evenly spaced lines along the outer rim of the circular knob. "Some kind of dial. You know, like the kind that might go on the outside of a servant bot's..." Elya trailed off and made a pulling gesture at his hip. "Container thingy."

"Cargo pocket?"

A snort tickled Elya's nose. "That's not what they're called."

"It's a pocket for cargo, isn't it?"

"If you say so." Elya had seen a bot struggling with such a compartment in its lower torso in this area of the station yesterday. Maybe the piece fell off of him. They were at the southeast point of the star, third level from the top. That bot had a knob just like the one. In fact, now that he gave it some thought, he'd found more odds and ends in the southern and eastern parts of the station than in other arms of the star. Only just now had his mind assimilated that information and recognized the pattern.

"What's that way?" Elya asked, pointing right at an intersection of two corridors. The chevron pattern on the floor angled left.

Arn scratched at his head. "I think that would take us to the hangar."

"Huh. I don't remember coming through this way."

"Me either. That first day was a blur."

After the encounter with Kristoph, Elya had endured the hours-long wait with a low fire of rage smoldering within him. The fury made his hands shake like an earthquake, so much so that his mother asked him if he was okay three or four times before she let him be. The anger sapped his strength and energy and soon his feet ached. After being stuck on the longhauler for three weeks, it had been an excruciating experience to stand for an entire day on a metal floor, shuffling slowly through the processing queue, in such an emotionally unstable state. By the time they were cleared and a pair of guards led them to their new room, the encounter with Kristoph had become like a bad dream. It haunted him, and he questioned all that had transpired.

The memory of this fugue state evaporated when a metallic gong echoed faintly down the corridor.

Elya inhaled sharply and lifted his head. The sound was the mental equivalent of getting cold water splashed on his face. "Did you hear that?"

Arn frowned and shook his head. Elya waited. An elderly couple carrying shopping bags, then a gaggle of teenagers, passed them in the narrow hall, filling the air with giggling and whispers. Arn and Elya stood to the side and waited until they all passed.

Gong.

Arn grinned. "I heard it that time."

The prospect of a treasure hunt already had Elya's feet flying. "This way!"

He ran down the hall, right at the intersection, then banked left into a sliding door, which retracted as he approached. As he passed through, the temperature dropped twenty degrees. They entered a large room lined with floor-to-ceiling shelves of vat-grown meats and cheeses, each separated by transparent panes of aluminite and individually temperature controlled. They had stumbled on a grocer's freezer. Each drawer was labeled with the name and logo of the producer. Judging by the notes, most of them were based on this station.

Elya and Arn passed through the grocery to an enormous hall beyond, which was honeycombed with dozens more shops of all kinds. They soon discovered that the honeycomb wrapped around the main hangar like a crescent around a moon. The walls and vaulted ceilings were all made of the same airy, 3d-printed foam material, cut with curved edges and supported by arch-like structures that lined the hall like the ribcage of some giant ocean monster. As a waystation between major star systems, it made perfect sense that Solaran's Bridge would need to be outfitted and supplied by a multitude of workers and goods. Elya had simply never thought through what that meant. In this area, people wearing the blue-grey uniforms of Solaran's Bridge staff ran about, busy as bees, while customers in a rainbow of brightly colored tunics, wearing soft shoes that would be no better than house slippers on Yuzosix, did their shopping.

The sound of the metallic gong grew louder as its ringing became less urgent. Elya knew he'd heard the sound before, but he wasn't sure until he caught sight of the huge dreadlocked man. The top half of his red jumpsuit now hung loose around his lean waist. Over the ropy muscles of his huge arms and barrel chest, he wore a tank top that clung sweatily to his frame. The man gave the metallic shell he was working on one last adjustment, banging out the remainder of a dent with a big hammer. Then he grabbed a rag hanging from his waist and buffed out a few marks before placing the shell over the complex innards of some kind of low-slung utility bot. It had a dozen kinds of brushes embedded in its base, so Elya figured the bot was some kind of cleaning machine. He fleetingly wondered if it could do much to combat the stench of unwashed refugees.

The man flipped a power switch hidden on its undercarriage and the bot whirled to life. It spun in circles, buzzed and beeped proudly, then zoomed around the shop, leaving a debris-free trail in its wake that was noticeable in the messy shop. Elya couldn't help but smile at the little bot's antics. A big grin split the machinist's face as well, somehow softening his image and making him seem approachable in Elya's eyes.

The man looked up and seemed to notice them for the first time. "How can I help you?"

"Uh," Elya stuttered. Now that the man's attention was on him, he suddenly felt self-conscious. His eyes darted around, looking for a reason to be here. A hand-painted sign strung along the back wall had *Welcome to the Chop Shop!* scrawled across it in red paint, to match the man's red jumpsuit. "I just... wondered..."

"My little brother loves bots," Arn said. Elya swallowed his stuttering attempt at a greeting, thankful for his big brother's smooth intervention.

The machinist in the red jumpsuit stepped forward, running the grease-spotted towel over his meaty paws. His eyes lit up as he came to some sort of epiphany, then reached out a hand. Elya allowed his own hand to be swallowed in the machinist's. "I recognize you," the man said. "From the hangar last week, during the big intake. It was a lucky thing they found your Mammoth. Drifting out there without comms, hiding in the darkness. You got real lucky." When he shook his hand, Elya felt as if his whole body was being pumped up and down.

He nodded. "Yeah."

"I'm Cormorant. You can call me Core. Hell of a thing y'all had to go through. I admire how you've bounced back so quickly. Some aren't so fortunate."

Elya hadn't really considered how his own resilience played a part, but Core had a good point. Elya thought of Rojer, who was bottling up more anger at the world than he ever had before.

"If you're not a refugee," Elya said, "what were you doing in the hangar that day?"

"Just helping out. I've got a skill that people are sorely in need of, especially during hard times. Doesn't harm me none to turn a wrench for free for a little while. Besides, there's been plenty of business since, from those who can afford it. It helped get the word out. I've been going nonstop since you got here." His smile tilted toward his right cheek, giving him a roguish look.

The taste of Elya's encounter with Kristoph was still bitter on his tongue. At the mention of 'those who can afford it', Elya looked over his shoulder, expecting to see the dull-knife smirk lurking behind him… but it was just his imagination as usual.

Core turned away and grabbed a circular canister

off a neat tool bench. He grabbed a pinch of something brown and stuffed it in his cheek as a teenage
girl came around the corner into the front of the
shop with her arms full of pipes and wires and other
bot parts. They were piled so high she couldn't see
where she was going and as she bumped into Arn,
the pile teetered. She gasped as they fell.

"Oh," she yelped. "Sorry! I'm so sorry!"

"It's okay," Arn said, smiling his broad, affable
smile as he bent down to help her pick up the pieces.

Arn could charm a powered-down bot with that
smile if he tried hard enough. Elya rolled his eyes.
The girl was near Arn's age and cute in a clumsy sort
of way, with long blond hair braided to the middle
of her back. Arn was already lovestruck. His older
brother whispered something that caused the girl to
laugh and roll her eyes at him.

Several cases of new and refurbished bot parts
drew Elya's attention away from them. There were
power switches, bolts, dials, knobs. Touchscreen and
hologram projectors. Plates with the Imperial
insignia on them. A whole basket contained about
six bazillion different kinds of wheels. Another case
showed off magnets for a variety of uses, half of
which Elya couldn't even fathom. His eyes fell on a
tool chest where different sizes and types of gears
were spread out. His breath caught in his chest at the
sight of a few of the gold-tinted ones. Somehow, it
was comforting to know that there were more gears

like the one Kristoph had stolen out there in the galaxy. Even if he couldn't have them.

In a corner, in a plastic case that featured a biometric lock on the top, were hundreds of carefully stored power cells and processors—the most treasured and expensive parts of the bots, if he was to believe the price lists he found on his tab the other day. He bit his lip and sighed. No matter how badly he wanted those pieces, he couldn't afford them and he wouldn't dream of stealing them from Core even if he could. It was one thing to gather spare parts from the floor of the station, to recover castoffs that other people had lost or left behind. It was quite another to take something that wasn't his, especially from a professional bot machinist who relied on them to make his living.

But, oh, how he wanted one...

Elya forced his eyes away from the locked case to a poster hanging on the back wall. Not one of the holograms that normally decorated the walls of a house or shop, but the old-fashioned kind made out of some sort of printed polymer. The poster showed a pilot standing next to his starfighter, sweat streaking his face and grinning with his helmet gripped in the crook of his elbow. The man had a tri-star insignia on his chest, the mark of the Solaran Empire and the Fleet. Char marks and debris scars decorated the front of the sleek plane behind him. A spider-like bot that came up to his knee was bouncing next to the pilot. The camera caught the bot in mid-jump, giving both he and the pilot a jubilant air.

"Good man, Captain Omar Ruidiaz," Core said. Elya hadn't heard the big man walk up behind him, but when he spoke Elya didn't jump. His voice was soothing. "We served together in the war. I learned my way around the inside of a bot as a starfighter mechanic while he flew his first missions."

Elya noticed the wistful tone in Core's voice. But only one thing interested him at this point. "Do all starfighter pilots have a bot of their own?"

"The smart ones do," Core said, "Fleet doesn't issue them, but if a bot meets the requirements they'll let a pilot bring them on missions. That one Ruidiaz built himself. With my help, of course."

Elya stared at Core, eyes lingering on the bulge of tabac stuffed into the man's cheek and the spark of mischief gleaming in his eyes. He realized that Core probably intimidated most people with his size. For some reason, Elya felt comfortable around the man. Something occurred to him, something he'd heard on the news or read on the cyclopedia somewhere.

"I thought most starfighters were operated remotely."

"No way. In the Yuzo chain, where you're from, maybe some are. It's a peaceful system… or it used to be." Elya pretended he hadn't heard that part. Core cleared his throat. "But on the front lines, you can't afford to rem-op a starfighter. Every nanosecond counts. Out there, a little lagtime can make the difference between life and death. That's why the job is volunteer only. Starfighter pilots need to be able to make peace with putting their lives at risk."

Core stopped talking and turned to a viewscreen nearby. He waved it on with a gesture, flipped through a file structure to find what he was looking for. The same starfighter Ruidiaz stood next to on the poster was suddenly twisting around a Kryl drone like a kamikaze maniac, doing barrel rolls and turns that made Elya's stomach lurch and twist. Everyone had heard the stories about starfighter pilots defending against the Kryl when they first encountered Solaran exploratory vessels a century ago. The war had been such a distant thing from his home on Yuzosix... but not anymore. Now it had become personal, and suddenly Elya wanted very badly to be in the cockpit of a starfighter himself, doing barrel rolls around Kryl drones and blasting their motherships to smithereens alongside Captain Ruidiaz and his spider.

To the stars with risk.

"Easy, kid," Core rumbled.

Elya slowly unclenched his fists. His breath was coming fast. Crescent-moon marks in his palms stung where his nails had dug in. He realized he hadn't been picturing a pinched Kryl face, but Kristoph's dull-knife smirk, in his mind.

"Listen," Core said. "I saw what happened in the hangar with that merchant's kid. I can't give back what he took from you... but maybe this will help."

Core stepped back behind the sales counters and reached down beside the locked case of power cells and processors. The spiky metal object he picked off a bottom shelf fit in the palm of his meaty fist. Elya felt his breath quickening again, this time with excitement and anticipation instead of anger. Core reached out and Elya felt himself instinctively open his hands—his heart caught in his throat.

It turned out to be a bot. Not a spare part or a discarded knob, but an *actual* bot! The miniature machine transformed before his eyes, expanding to twice its original size as its legs unfolded and its body unfurled, turning from a spiky metal ball to a small hedgehog. Elya realized Core must have activated the bot as he dropped it into his hands. The spikes were actually hundreds of hair-thin polymer bristles, and it seemed to sniff his palm as Elya squatted down to set it gently on the floor.

"It can smell?" he asked.

"In a sense. Every bot is purpose-built. This one was designed to detect danger in hostile new environments. First, it takes a sample of your DNA. Then, it can test anything it encounters against your genetic code—other materials and objects, plants, liquids, even gases. The Fleet uses them on missions of planetary exploration to measure atmospheric composition, detect poisons in the water supply, that sort of thing."

The hedgehog explored outward from Elya, "sniffing" around him in ever-expanding circles. It was so quick, Elya felt like he could only track the bot in frames. A blue underglow trailed wherever it went so that Elya had no trouble following him when it disappeared into the back of Core's shop and crawled beneath a curved aluminite plate. When the hedgehog completed his exploration and returned to Elya, its lights blinked green three times. Elya bent down and let the bot crawl back into his hand.

"Green means all clear. If it blinks red, that's when you need to watch out." Core winked at him from his full, towering height. "You can read more about these models on your tab. Model number CL-454."

Elya nodded mutely and turned his rapt attention back to the tiny bot. It didn't seem real, to hold a bot of his very own in his hand. *CL-454. A hedgehog bot. Hedgebot.* All of a sudden, a guilt complex over-whelmed him. He held the bot out to Core. "He belongs to you. I can't afford to buy him."

"Nah," Core scoffed, "Don't sweat it. I've got enough bots to take care of. You take care of that one for me, okay?"

Elya nodded dumbly and swallowed against a dryness in his throat. He was overwhelmed—by the

idea of having his own bot for the first time, by
Core's generosity, by the tragedy that had upended
his life and his family. It took a tremendous effort to
hold the tears back so this man he respected, this
generous stranger, didn't see him cry.

He kept his face turned away while nodding
emphatically and cupping the tiny bot to his breast.
Core seemed to understand, and went back to his
work repairing bots beneath the *Welcome to the Chop
Shop!* sign.

Arn was deep in conversation with the girl. She
had put her arms back through the sleeves of a tan
jumpsuit. The garb, along with the bot parts she had
been caring, cemented the fact that she worked for
the burly machinist. Maybe she was his apprentice.
Elya burned with questions for her, about what it
was like to work with bots.... but his brother was
obviously enamored with the girl, hanging onto her
every word while he wore a rapt expression Elya
only saw on Arn's face under one condition.

Elya decided to give them some space.

Saying nothing, he turned and wandered out of
Core's store, curious what else this honeycomb of
shops had to offer. He held his breath, waiting for
Arn to call after him, to warn him not to wander too
far. The warning never came. Elya carried Hedgebot
past an Imperial bank terminal, then by a dry goods
store, then a weapons dealer, before he decided to
experiment and set Hedgebot down for a bit. The

mechanical creature surged ahead. Elya smiled help-lessly as he followed the little bot through the halls. He noticed that Hedgebot never moved more than about twenty meters apart from him. Elya would have to do some research to find out if that was programmed in, and if he had any control over the length of the invisible tether. Despite this ineresting observation, his heart leapt into his throat when Hedgebot disappeared around a corner and behind a set of stairs.

There was a hidden storage area tucked away back here, a nook with no door where a bunch of lightweight folding chairs and extra tables had been stacked against the wall. But that was not what initially caught Elya's attention. Hedgebot had stopped just under the stairway, at the mouth of an open door. The halo of light around the bot had darkened to yellow and was slowly burning toward a red-tinted orange.

It only took a moment to see why. Elya froze. He didn't dare breathe and it was a good thing his new bot didn't have to. At the back of the storage room, three boys Arn's age surrounded a humanoid bot with a golden casing. One of the boys had a dull-knife smirk that was currently separated into a sharp-edged grin of maniacal proportions. This time the sight wasn't Elya's imagination or his mind playing tricks. It was Kristoph, in the flesh and blood.

The three boys didn't immediately notice Elya or his little danger-scouting Hedgebot for two reasons: One, Elya crouched in the shadow of the staircase. And two, they were too busy abusing the bot trapped between them to look around.

When Elya's mind snapped back into action, he came to his senses and took three steps backward, out of Kristoph's line of sight.

"Hedgebot!" Elya whispered. "Come back!"

The hedgehog twisted its head to look back at him, but didn't move away from the doorframe. Its underglow darkened another shade.

Elya felt his heart slam repeatedly into his ribcage. His chest expanded and contracted rapidly. His palms, splayed against a metallic wall, left sweaty streaks where he pressed.

"Master, I do not understand," a servant bot's familiar electronic voice pleaded in a worried tone. The bot sounded distraught. A metallic crunch reverberated through the cracked door. This time it wasn't the siren call of the Chop Shop, but a clamor far more sinister.

"Shut up, Ambit," Kristoph snapped.

A hollow thump sounded as someone struck the bot again. Elya flinched at the sound.

"Your father would not approve." Ambit scolded Kristoph as if he were a child. Such a tone would have worked on Elya.

"I said, *shut up!*" This time the noise was not a simple thud, but a *rip-tear-crunch*.

Ambit did not respond. The silence was deafening. Still frightened, but now filled with a terrible curiosity, Elya ventured a peek around the corner. Ambit's arm lay on the floor. The gold-skinned servant bot bent to retrieve it. He slowly picked up his arm and gazed at it with a cocked head, as if something was severely out of order but he couldn't quite fathom what.

Elya let his whole weight fall against the wall. He was overcome with a surprisingly forceful—yet clearly insane—desire to rush out to Ambit, grab his severed arm and lead him back to Core to get repaired. Only an equally strong desire not to relive the helpless rage he'd felt facing Kristoph in the hangar kept him magnetized to the spot.

Hedgebot had gone full red now, a color brighter and more dangerous than Imperial crimson. He had curled up into a tight knot. Shelled in like that, there was no way it would be able to come back to Elya on its own, at least not until he figured out how to control it properly. Did the bot need some sort of remote? Could he connect it to his tab?

The dull-knife smirk turned in Elya's direction, noticing the glowing red hedgehog, and then catching a glimpse of Elya himself.

Elya whipped his body backward, but he knew it was too late. He thought about bolting, but he couldn't bear to let them take Hedgebot. Elya would die inside if they did to his bot what they had just done to do to poor Ambit.

Easy, little brother. Arn's voice came to him unbidden. Elya was still terrified, but the mental voice of his brother steeled him just enough to face what he had to do.

Elya darted out, scooped up Hedgebot in his hands, and sprinted all the way back to their little cabin at the north point of the station.

He'd never run so fast in his life.

4

From the moment he ran scared from Kristoph like a dog with his tail between his legs, Elya fought an internal war with himself. On the one side was a potent desire to return to Core's shop, to learn more about bots and starfighter pilots—how to care for the former and whether it was possible for a humble farm boy from Yuzosix who collected bot parts to become the latter. Core's kindness and insight had opened a new galaxy of possibilities for Elya. At a time when the universe seemed intent on shattering any coherent vision of his own future, Core had given him a dose of hope.

On the other side was a blood-chilling cocktail of fear and shame. Fear for his safety, and shame for running scared. Core wouldn't have run scared from Kristoph, and neither would Captain Ruidiaz or even his brother Arn. Elya had been beaten up by bullies before, but something about the way Kristoph and his friends had laughed while Ambit was picking up his arm and trying to figure out what had gone wrong frightened him more than your average gang of bullies with three-to-one odds would have.

So, although he explored other parts of the station with Arn, over the next several days Elya steadfastly steered clear of the area near the hangar.

And then suddenly the Nevers were informed that it was time to depart.

"Already?" Elya asked.

"Finally," Rojer said, as if his younger sibling hadn't spoken. "I thought we'd be stuck here forever."

"It was less time than we spent on the Mammoth," Elya pointed out as he pulled on his rucksack and cinched the straps tight. Hedgebot ran along his shoulders and disappeared below the flap into the rucksack. The little dude loved walking all over Elya's arms and shoulders, and hiding in the pack. In just a few short days, the pokey metal claws had become as familiar a sensation to Elya as his nails against his own skin.

Rojer stared daggers at Elya, who cast his eyes downward reflexively and then was immediately mad that Rojer still seemed to have that power over him. He forced himself to lift his chin and meet his brother's eyes.

"Shut up," Rojer said.

"Make me," Elya retorted.

"Hush, both of you," Mom said. "Keep packing."

Elya did as he was told and after a minute so did Rojer, complaining the whole while. Except for Hedgebot, they hadn't acquired many things during their stay on Solaran's Bridge, so it only took a few minutes. Together, the Nevers clan made their way back toward the hangar. The closer they got, the more Elya fidgeted. Pretending his hands were infinite steps, he guided the restless hedgehog in an endless circular climb.

"Please, stop," Mom said, "you're making me dizzy, and I need you to pay attention to where you're going."

Elya did as he was told, though it took an effort of will power to still his hands. He missed the comforting weight of the golden gear in his pocket. If he couldn't play with Hedgebot, he had nothing to fidget with.

Near the hangar, their forward motion stalled as they came up against a crowd in the main corridor. They waited for the crowd to clear, shuffling forward with the rest of the refugees who had been cleared to leave today. Knowing they were in the east wing of the star-shaped space station, near the hangar, Elya's heart pitter-pattered in his chest.

"Remember, stick together," Mom said. She looked each of the boys in the eye, and they nodded their acknowledgment in turn. Her eyes lingered on Elya, and he felt his cheeks heat up. But this time she didn't say it. She didn't have to.

Don't wander off.

That thought combined with the crowded hallway triggered a memory, one he'd instinctually buried. Elya's palms began to sweat as his heart picked up speed. Suddenly, he was back on Yuzosix, at the spaceport where all residents had been told to go to evacuate the planet. There was one in the city near their home, but in the crowded rush of everyone trying to get there from hundreds of miles in *every* direction, it had taken them a full day and a half to reach the spaceport. By the time they arrived, Elya was exhausted, and the terminal itself had been overflowing with people. His mother had tried to be polite, had tried to wait their turn, but it was pure chaos and they had been forced to push their way onto the shuttle or risk being left behind.

"Stick together!" Mom had yelled over the raucous din as she pressed into the crowd.

Despite his best efforts, Elya got separated from his family. He had looked up just as Rojer disappeared ahead of him, and Arn, usually bringing up the rear, had somehow gotten in front of Elya without noticing he'd passed his brother. All of a sudden Elya was alone, practically invisible and underfoot in the crowd. Someone shoved him, he tripped and—

Arn touched his shoulder, causing Elya to jump and turn, squeezing Hedgebot to his chest.

"Easy, little brother," he said.

Elya sucked air through his nostrils, which seemed constricted and tight, like he was breathing through coffee straws. He closed his eyes, opening his mouth to gulp air, and forced himself to relax. The crowd was thick here, but this was the space station, not the spaceport terminal on Yuzosix. He was safe. He was safe.

Guided by Arn's gentle hands on his shoulders, Elya moved ahead slowly. Eventually they passed through a threshold into the hangar, and the crowd dissipated, or at least spread out into the larger space.

People were scattered everywhere, just as they had been on the day of their arrival, only this time, lines formed at the airlock entrances rather than the door into the station. None of the airlocks had been opened yet, though, nor did the Nevers know which one they were supposed to use. Elya's mother found an empty spot of floor and swung her pack down.

"I'm going to find out which ship we've been assigned to," she said as she rubbed her shoulders. "And grab a few supplies. You all wait here."

"Can I go with you?" Elya asked.

"No, honey, I'll just be a minute."

"Take him with you, then," Elya said holding out his bot. It was glowing blue now, but if she ran into danger, it would warn her better than anything else. "He'll keep you safe."

"Thanks sweetie, but I'll be fine."

She turned and vanished into the crowd.

Rojer rolled his eyes at Elya, pulled his tab out of his pack, and began to watch videos to pass the time, slyly picking his nose when he thought no one was looking (they were).

Elya set Hedgebot down and watched it roam, the blue light glowing beneath its belly and lighting the grated floor of the hangar as it darted back and forth, scouting, seeking, searching.

"Hey little fella," a girl said, bending over to stroke Hedgebot's back. It was the blond from Core's shop, the one Arn had a crush on. In the time since meeting her, Elya had learned her name was Norah. "How are you getting along with our favorite little danger detector?"

Arn straightened next to him and shared a genuine smile with Norah. While Elya had avoided the area around the hangar in recent days, Arn had not, taking advantage of every opportunity he wasn't tasked with watching after Elya to sneak off and visit with his new girlfriend.

"He's great," Elya said honestly. "I just wish I knew how to get him to come back to me after he finds something that scares him."

"Oh, that's not too hard," Norah said, putting a finger to her mouth. "Hm, let's see...come stand over here for me." Elya did as she suggested. Norah waited while Hedgebot came around, then set a foot gently down on top of it, putting her weight gently down until it started to squirm. The light below it didn't change from blue, but it immediately curled up into a knot of metal.

"If it encounters danger for you, it turns red. If it runs into danger for itself, it generally curls into a ball. If either of these things happen, a simple snap of your fingers or a whistle will bring it back to you. Assuming it's not stuck."

Elya tried snapping. His first attempt barely made any sound, but on his second attempt he managed to make a bit of a pop. At the same time, Norah let up her foot. Hedgebot uncurled, scampered over to Elya, and crawled up until it sat on his shoulder.

"Wow, cool! Thanks."

"Sure thing. Mind if I borrow your brother for a second?"

Elya nodded. Norah took Arn by the hand and dragged him away. Elya rolled his eyes behind their back, but Arn only had eyes for the girl and didn't notice his youngest brother's contempt.

Unfortunately, that left Elya alone with Rojer, who he had no desire to spend any time with. He'd suffered enough of Rojer's badgering in front of the others and knew that it would be worse alone. Elya immediately set Hedgebot back down and moved a few yards away from his brother.

"Mom said wait here."

"What?" Elya said. "I can't hear you over the sound of you picking your nose." Rojer grimaced, mumbled something under his breath, and turned his back on his brother as he went back to watching videos.

This gave Elya the perfect opportunity to gain a healthy distance from his brother. He was careful to keep one eye on Rojer, and the other on Arn and Norah, who had ducked into a shadowy corner and were now making out and murmuring sweet nothings in each other's ears. Arn looked up once and caught his little brother's eye, and Elya immediately turned away as he felt his face heat up. When he first realized Arn's relationship with this girl had become serious, Elya had only felt annoyance and disgust. She was taking his brother away from him, after all. Now, for the first time, he felt it for what it truly was... jealousy.

Distracted by these strange and foreign feelings, Elya lost sight of Hedgebot. He found the blue light in the threshold of a doorway that led to the honeycomb of shops hugging the large hangar in a crescent-moon embrace. Butterflies flapped in his stomach at the idea of disobeying his mother, of sneaking away again, out of Arn's line of sight. But there were a lot of people out there, shopping. He would be safe in the crowd, wouldn't he? And with his reliable little danger detector at his side, what could go wrong?

Elya followed the tiny bot, who scampered into the hive of shops as he approached, always staying ten or twenty meters ahead of him, by design. Elya knew that he could turn around and go back to rejoin Rojer at any point, and that Hedgebot would follow him. But he chose not to. It felt good to face his fears. Scary, but good. He began to rehearse a conversation with Core in his head. The Chop Shop had been just around the corner to the left, hadn't it?

His mental rehearsal was interrupted when he caught sight of Hedgebot's blue light reflecting off a shiny object sitting in a hole in the airy, curved wall. He walked toward it, wiping his sweaty palms on his pants and trying to keep hold of the reigns on his excitement. It was a bot part, he saw as he approached, and one he'd never had in his possession before: a finger with two joints. The metal shell had a bluish tint that he'd only seen once or twice—a rare color. Elya took the lone digit and dropped it into his pocket, looking around to be sure no one had noticed him taking it. Streams of people walked by in the hall, each of them busy with their own objectives, bearing armfuls of bags and supplies for their upcoming journeys.

Hedgebot's blue light drifted forward. Elya noticed another metal digit in another hole in the wall further down the hall. He could have sworn he'd looked at that empty hole just a minute ago, but as the crowd passed he looked again and saw the metallic shine. Another finger. When he picked this one up, Hedgebot seemed to catch on to what he was doing. Elya found four fingers in the space of a few minutes, and was distracted thinking that perhaps Core would have a hand on which to mount them, when he reached the end of the shopping area.

He'd been so distracted by imagining the construction of his bot hand that he didn't notice he'd come to the end of the hall. There were no stairs at this end, but there were a few empty shops, gated by vertical garage-like doors that pulled down from above. Hedgebot went still, but its light stayed blue, indicating to Elya that there was no danger here.

Why, then, had the muscles in his neck and shoulders gone all tense?

"I knew he'd fall for the bait," someone said from behind him. "So predictable."

Turning around, Elya's stomach sank into his feet as he looked into a familiar dull-knife smirk.

One of the two bullies that had been with Kristoph when they ripped off Ambit's arm moved in behind him and lifted the sliding garage door that led to one of the empty shops. Kristoph and the other bully stepped forward, forcing Elya inside. His blood went cold, and the warring emotions of fear and shame flooded through his body. He fought to stay calm, but his heart hammered rapidly, his palms sweated, and his breathing became shallow.

Ambit stood inside the empty shop with his arms at his sides and his chin slumped onto his concave golden chest. The arm that had been torn off had been reattached—poorly. It hung down at a weird angle that made Elya certain it hadn't been done by Core or any kind of professional. The other arm ended at the wrist in a clump of frayed wires. No hand at all. The servant bot was on power-saving mode. Elya didn't know how they'd gotten the key to this empty shop, but he figured that Kristoph's merchant father had some weight with the shop-keeper's union, or maybe Kristoph and his friends had broken in. It didn't matter. Elya was trapped here with them, a thought that was cemented when they let the door fall closed, then flipped on some dim lights. If Elya ran for freedom now, that would only encourage them, make the punishment come faster. So he stood his ground. Hedgebot swirled around his feet. His light was still blue, but warming toward orange. No outright danger detected—at least not yet. The bot was useful, but for this kind of threat, it was clear that Elya's senses were more evolved.

"Did you get so bored torturing your poor bot that you have to pick on *me* now?" Elya demanded in a voice that quivered in the air of the empty shop.

"We were just having a little fun," Kristoph said. "Ambit can't feel anything. Isn't that right, Ambit?"

Ambit powered up and lifted his head to regard Kristoph with unlit eyes. "Yes, Master Kristoph," Ambit said. "I am a bot and do not experience physical pain."

What had they done to the poor bot? His defeated posture was like a knife to Elya's heart. And the missing hand...

Elya took his own hand out of his pocket, where he'd been unconsciously clutching the bot digits for comfort. Looking down, he noticed that his palm and fingers were wet and blue, as if he'd touched a freshly painted wall. He pulled out one of the bot digits and saw that the color had come off where his sweaty hands had been nervously rubbing the knuckle in his pocket. Beneath the fresh coat of blue paint, the original gold shone dully through.

Disgusted with his own gullibility, Elya removed all four metal fingers and tossed them at Ambit's feet with a mumbled, "Sorry."

Ambit bent down and gathered the fingers in his remaining hand, then stood and powered off again. Every bit the obedient machine.

"Sorry?" Kristoph scowled. "The only thing you have to be sorry for is how you embarrassed me in front of my father."

As he stepped into the nimbus of warming orange light cast by Hedgebot, Elya noticed that there was a deep reddish-purple bruise around Kristoph's left eye. Several smaller bruises mottled his upper arms, and Elya had the distinct impression, though he couldn't prove it, that the bruises had been caused by his father's angry hands.

Whatever pity Elya felt for the older boy was immediately trampled by a deep-seated sense of injustice that came bubbling forth, forming words before he could think to filter them.

Unable to help himself, Elya shouted, "You stole the gear from me! If you were embarrassed, you brought it on yourself."

Hedgebot's warning glow flashed from orange to fireball red, sending Elya's senses into overdrive. Time seemed to slow down. He reacted on instinct, leaning backward as something sharp and metallic sliced toward him in an arc.

If it wasn't for the split-second warning from Hedgebot, Elya never would have made it out of that room alive. But he did get the advantage of the warning, which is why the blade of Kristoph's pocket knife grazed his cheek instead of opening his throat.

He barely felt the cut. The knife's edge slid across his right cheekbone as he stepped backward and tripped over the boot of one of the other bullies, a heavy-set kid with curly hair and a condescending sneer that followed him to the floor. Elya landed and rolled and kept rolling, having learned from wrestling with his brothers that if you get a chance to gain some distance from your attackers, you better take it. He came up in a kneeling position, one knee on the ground, the other leg supporting his weight, facing Kristoph and bracing for a rush attack. That's how Rojer would have played it.

But Kristoph was far more cunning than his brother. Elya panted hard, his heart pounding in his ears. He braced for an attack—none came. Instead, Kristoph leaned his weight on Hedgebot, who was stuck under one oiled leather boot.

"This is a neat little bot," Kristoph purred. "Where'd you get him?"

"He's mine! You let him go right now."

"Or what? You'll bleed on me?" He chuckled along with the other boys. The heavyset bully to Kristoph's right—the one that had tripped Elya— bent down and twisted one of Hedgebot's metallic claws, trying to pry it off. The hedgehog quickly curled into its defensive ball position. The other kid, a boy of Arn's age with long blond hair and a gaunt, underfed face circled slowly around, trying to get an angle on him.

Elya eyeballed the other boys as he raised a hand to the cut on his cheek, wiping away the wetness he felt there. Blood mixed with the blue paint in his palm, merging into a deep purple smudge in the dim light of the empty shop. He was still panting hard and scared stiff, but this time Elya refused to run. He wouldn't—he couldn't—leave his bot to suffer at the hands of Kristoph the way Ambit had. Bots couldn't die, and according to Ambit they didn't feel pain the way people did... but that hardly seemed to matter. Core had placed Hedgebot into Elya's care. Whatever happened to it was his responsibility now.

With a nod from Kristoph, the two bullies lumbered forward and began to pummel Elya with their fists. Their blows rained down like the worst hail storms on Yuzosix, and he had no shelter under which to hide. Elya tried to fight back, but he was too small and they were too strong. It took all his strength merely to keep his arms up to protect his face. They took advantage of every opening to bruise his ribs, kick him in the shins and beat him into the ground until he was curled into a ball like his bot.

Every time he tried to get up, they'd trip him and shove him down again. There were only two of them, but it reminded him so much of his flight from Yuzosix, of getting lost in the maddened crowd, that the feeling of powerlessness he'd felt then came rushing back. Tears wet his face even as they continued to beat him.

When they finally got bored of kicking him, the thin bully and the heavyset one lifted him beneath his armpits and dragged him over to where Kristoph was shoving his pocketknife into Hedgebot's protective ball in an attempt to pry it open. This lit a fire in

Elya. Despite the throbbing pain that filled his body, the sight of Kristoph torturing his bot renewed his determination. He vowed not to let them see how afraid he was.

"Make him open," Kristoph demanded.

Elya lifted his tear-streaked face and spit a mouthful of blood at Kristoph. It felt *good* to watch the older boy's face contort with fury.

"That's it! You're going to watch while I grind him into stardust!"

Elya thrashed in their grip, but the bullies held him tight. He was forced to watch while Kristoph smashed the heel of his boot down on Hedgebot over and over and over again. Still, this didn't seem to cause any harm to the bot—it was a sturdy little machine, built to endure danger and harm. Seeing that his efforts were ineffective, Kristoph tried his knife again, and when that didn't work, he found a heavy metal cabinet shoved in the corner of the office and made Ambit drag it over to him with his one good hand. The cabinet screeched as it scraped across the metal floor. And then Kristoph shoved it over and slammed it down on Hedgebot until its outer shell cracked.

"Hah!" Kristoph shouted in triumph, bending down and picking up his pocket knife once more. In a flash, Elya knew how they'd removed Ambit's hand and cut the frayed wires in his arm. Elya struggled harder in the grip of the two bullies. He could hear the breath of the heavyset one coming hard and fast in his left ear. They were getting tired from giving the beating and their sweaty hands were beginning to slip on his arms.

Elya leaned as far forward as he could, angling down toward Hedgebot. The bullies hands slipped down to his wrists. He lunged backward and thrust his body upward, bashing his head into the fat bully's double chin. The older boy cried out and released Elya's arm. He didn't look to see what kind of damage he'd caused, but he would have bet that the warm wet droplets that splattered the back of his neck weren't water. He used the leverage he now had to twist around, causing the thin bully holding his other arm to cuss and scrabble for a better grip. Elya's knee in his groin finally caused him to release the hold on his wrist.

So intent was he on trying to shove his knife into Hedgebot's innards that Kristoph didn't immediately move to help his companions. But when Elya came after him, Kristoph finally turned, slashing his knife out at him again in anger. This time Elya anticipated it. He hopped backward and the knife caught in his shirt, entangling the two of them and momentarily capturing the little pocket knife. Elya felt the cold blade against his skin and twisted, trying to get away from the sharp edge and failing. He was stuck. Kristoph sneered and seethed, spittle bubbling between his clenched teeth and spraying into Elya's face. But Elya was just as angry now as Kristoph was. No one attacked his bot and got away with it.

He grabbed the hand Kristoph used to hold the knife and forced it away from his own chest. They struggled like this, pushing and pulling each other until Kristoph got his feet tangled in the legs of the thin bully, who was still groaning and clutching his groin on the ground.

When Elya felt Kristoph stumble, he shoved outward and released his hold on Kristoph's knife-hand. Expecting resistance from Elya and finding none, Kristoph fell backward, windmilling his arms and throwing the pocketknife across the room. His hip slammed against the metal cabinet he'd used to crack Hedgebot's protective shell. He used his hands, now empty, to brace himself against the cabinet—and suddenly began to seize.

Elya inhaled sharply through his nose and felt his eyes go wide. He and the two bullies watched, jaws gaping, as Kristoph shook with powerful tremors. Smoke began to rise from where his palms met the metal cabinet. Terrified and confused, Elya gathered his wits and sprinted to the side of the room, where the pocket knife had landed. He picked up the knife, turned—and that's when he finally understood what was happening.

Kristoph shook like he was having a seizure, his whole body rocking back and forth. His hands were stuck to the cabinet as if they'd been glued there. The frayed wires in Ambit's severed wrist were touching the side of the cabinet, infusing it with electrical energy. That energy flowed from Ambit's power source, through the cabinet, and into Kristoph through his hands, electrocuting him.

Sparks lit the room when Ambit finally removed the frayed wires trailing out of his wrist from the metal side of the cabinet. His eyes lit up. The bot turned his head toward Elya and nodded, almost imperceptibly. Then his chin fell to his chest as the light faded from his eyes, and he powered off completely, his power cells depleted.

Kristoph slumped and fell to the ground with a thud. He didn't move.

Bearing the knife in front of him toward the two bullies—who, while not unconscious like Kristoph, were still dangerous—Elya stepped over to Kristoph's side. The bullies watched him but didn't interfere. Whether they were afraid of Ambit, now, or afraid of the knife he held, Elya neither knew nor cared.

Using his free hand, he carefully collected Hedgebot. The red light went cold and faded to a pale blue at his touch. He set the bot aside, then, gathering his courage, Elya reached into Kristoph's tunic and felt around. He sighed in relief when his hands came into contact with a familiar set of finely cut teeth. Elya removed the golden gear that

Kristoph had stolen, and stowed it carefully in his own pocket.

Picking up Hedgebot in one hand, and bearing the pocket knife in the other, Elya backed slowly out of the room, keeping the other boys in his sight until he bumped into the door. Kristoph remained unconscious with smoke curling in the air above him. The other two clutched their wounds. Crouching on trembling legs, Elya hauled the door up with his knife hand and slipped away.

5

Wrung out and ragged, bruised and beaten, Elya stumbled into Rojer and Arn, who had been running madly around the hangar and through the shops, frantically searching for him.

They shouted with joy when he collapsed into their arms—even Rojer seemed happy to see his little brother—and then demanded to know what had happened.

Elya didn't want to talk about it. He cradled Hedgebot and cried silently. But when his mother came back and saw the state Elya was in, with his cut cheek and bruised body and battered bot, she absolutely lost it. Elya was forced to explain what happened just to get her to calm down and stop raging in front of everyone. An audience of gawking people had gathered, and all Elya wanted at that moment was to get out of their sight.

Instead of calming his mother down, his story seemed to enrage her. She dragged Elya in front of a pair of security guards and demanded that Kristoph and the other boys be taken into custody and charged with assault.

Elya didn't object. They deserved it. But he was too tired to show much enthusiasm. Elya led the guards to the empty shop. Neither Kristoph nor the other boys were to be found. But the blood-spattered evidence was all over the floor, and Ambit was still there, handless and unresponsive next to the cabinet, standing with his head lolling forward and no sign of life in his eyes.

If servant bots weren't built to look like people, perhaps it wouldn't have affected Elya so deeply. As it was, the depressing sight of the tortured bot sent him spiraling. He retreated to a corner and sank to the ground with his back to the wall. "He's gone catatonic!" one of the guards said when Elya failed to respond to a string of inane questions.

Adults could be real idiots sometimes.

"I already told you what happened!" Elya said. "Can't you see? Just leave me alone."

"I think that's quite enough," Mom said, stepping in front of Elya and forcing the guards to give him some space. That his mother defended him and didn't heap blame on him for wandering off—though, of course, he did—was the kindest thing she had ever done. Elya had never loved and admired her more than in that moment. Nor had he ever felt so guilty for disobeying her.

An investigative unit was called in. After a few hours, Kristoph and his confederates were located. Kristoph had woken up and stumbled back to his parents' cabin, where his father had been hiding the boy, and lying to the investigators. The other two were discovered cowering together in a storage room.

The investigator told his mother that the boys would be punished, which seemed to satisfy her. She let them know she'd be checking to make sure Kristoph's father didn't find some way to get the Imperial Inquisitor to lessen their sentences, or conveniently "dismiss" the case.

"It's in the Empire's hands now, ma'am," the investigator replied.

When it was all over, Elya was relieved to learn that the whole ordeal had caused Kristoph to be placed on a different Mammoth longhauler. They were forced to stay behind for an Inquisitor to project in on the Ansible network and pass their sentence, while the Nevers were allowed to go.

"Please, can I take Hedgebot to Core to get fixed? Please, Mom. I'm begging you."

Hedgebot beeped sadly in Elya's arms.

"We don't have time, hun. They've already delayed their departure for us. We'll get the bot fixed when we get to the settlement, I promise."

As luck would have it, word of what happened reached Core. Elya's heart soared when he saw the machinist and his blond assistant waiting for him at the mouth of the airlock. Core handed Elya a heavy bag. It had the tri-star insignia of the Solaran Empire printed on both sides.

"That's a machinist's repair kit. I just transferred an instruction manual to your tab. You'll do fine if you just follow the instructions."

Norah and Arn embraced and whispered a tearful goodbye. Core looked at the two of them and smiled sadly.

"Will Hedgebot be okay?" Elya asked.

"Don't worry, kid," Core said, "Any damage to a bot can be repaired with the right parts and enough patience."

Elya took a deep, trembling breath and let it out. All of his fear and shame seemed to be expelled with it. He thanked Core, and then followed his brothers and mother through the airlock and onto the Mammoth that would take them to their new home.

6

Ever since they became refugees, Elya Nevers collected bot parts.

He didn't know when this habit had formed, or how the idea had first come to him. But it didn't matter. It was a part of him now. Elya Nevers collected bot parts. It was who he was.

And not just bot *parts*. Elya, who grew up poor on a rural solar farm and had never been able to afford a bot of his own, now had Hedgebot, a danger detector all his own. A bot who had saved his life.

It took him several weeks to repair Hedgebot. Fortunately, the trip to their new home took longer, so he had plenty of uninterrupted time to focus on the problem. He read the instruction manual from beginning to end, watched every video twice, and practiced on his bot and any other spare parts he could find until his fingers ached.

The many spare parts he'd been collecting came in handy. Using a small welder and other tools he found in the repair kit Core gave him, along with the parts he had collected and a few more he scrounged together on the new Mammoth, Elya was able to restore the bot's broken outer shell.

"I'm proud of you," Mom said as she watched the bot scurry happily around the room, curling into a ball and uncurling several times as he tested his newly repaired defensive function. "You worked hard on that."

"Pretty incredible, little brother," Arn said.

They all turned to Rojer. "Yeah, it's all right, I guess."

Elya burst out laughing and threw his arms around Rojer. "I love you, brother. Even if you are a grump."

Rojer groaned. "Are we there yet?"

Elya craned his head around and stared off through a porthole into the black expanse of space, mottled with stars. He spotted a giant orange marble in the distance, around which several settler's moons were said to orbit. "Actually, it looks like we are."

Elya snapped his fingers and Hedgebot scurried up his leg and perched on his shoulder. The Nevers family crowded around the porthole and watched as they drifted closer to their new home.

Keep reading to learn about *Starfighter Down*, Elya's next big adventure.

———————————

Sign up for MG's newsletter for release announcements and more insider-only content!

STARFIGHTER DOWN

Elya's story continues in the first full length novel of the *Relics of the Ancients* space opera series!

Space battles, murderous xenos, ancient relics with mysterious power, and much more in this interstellar action adventure.

Order *Starfighter Down* today!

ALSO BY M.G. HERRON

TRANSLOCATOR TRILOGY

1. The Auriga Project

2. The Alien Element

3. The Ares Initiative

Panic at the Tomb (Short Story)

The Translocator (Trilogy Box Set)

THE GUNN FILES

1. Culture Shock

2. Overdose

3. Quantum Flare

OTHER BOOKS

The Republic

Boys & Their Monsters

Get science fiction and fantasy reading recommendations from MG Herron delivered straight to your inbox. Join here: mgherron.com/bookclub

M.G. Herron writes science fiction and fantasy for adrenaline junkies.

His books explore new worlds, futuristic technologies, ancient mysteries, various apocalypses, and the vagaries of the human experience.

His characters have a sense of humor (except for the ones who don't). They stand up to strange alien monsters from other worlds... unless they slept through their alarm again.

Like ordinary people, Herron's heroes sometimes make mistakes, but they're always trying to make the universe a better place.

Find all his books and news about upcoming releases at mgherron.com.

Made in the USA
Monee, IL
24 July 2021